THE ADVENTURES OF

ROWENA

AND
THE WONDERFUL JAM AND JELLY FACTORY

A CHILDREN'S STORY COOKBOOK

To my very special father,
without whose love, devotion and eternal
support the magic of life would not have touched
the real Jam and Jelly Factory. The thrill of living life to
its fullest with optimism and wonderment, caring and sharing
is his most cherished gift to me. My fondest hope is
that the children who share these adventures and special
tastes will feel my father's contribution and thereby
share the joy and zest for life he has given me.

Very special thanks . . .
to Sigrid Couch of Kaye Taylor & Associates who perceived the essence of
my concept and directed the super support team which produced this book.
to Cameron Foster for her creative cooking talents with the recipes.
to Wilma Clark for her artistic eye in graphic design.
to Sharon Knapp for her ability to edit from a child's perspective.

Story copyright © 1987 by Rowena Jaap
Illustrations copyright © 1987 by Deborah G. Rogers

Designed by Clark Design Studio

A Children's Story-Cookbook Series
Published by Stanley Press, Inc.

Printed by S.C. Toof and Company, Memphis, Tennessee

First Printing
Library of Congress Catalog Card Number: 87-62189
ISBN: 0-944345-11-5

THE ADVENTURES OF
ROWENA
AND
THE WONDERFUL JAM AND JELLY FACTORY

Written by Rowena Jaap
Illustrated by Deborah G. Rogers

STANLEY PRESS, INC.
POST OFFICE BOX 11101
NORFOLK, VIRGINIA 23517

Once upon a time, there had been a wonderful Jam and Jelly Factory at the end of the road.

It had been a busy, magical place. But now it stood silent and empty.

Rowena's family had just moved into her grandmother's old house and she had wandered down the road to see if she could find the factory again.

Rowena could still see the old sign above the door:

The name was the same, for her very own grandmother had built the factory. The sign brought back marvelous memories of delicious smells and good things to eat. Rowena could still remember it all from when she was very little.

As she walked slowly up the path, Rowena thought, "I wonder what it looks like inside? Maybe I could fix it up. This is going to be a real adventure."

As Rowena started to push the door open, she noticed a very dignified gentleman mouse standing there. She quickly drew her hand back from the door and said,

"Hello! I'm Rowena and this was my grandmother's jam and jelly factory. Who are you?"

And without taking a breath, "Do you think it would be all right for me to go in?"

"Just a minute, young lady! Only one question at a time." The mouse stood up as tall as he could, puffed twice on his pipe and pushed his glasses up on his nose.

"I am Mr. Jellyfords Jam III, but you may call me Mr. Jam. And yes, but of course, you may come in. Your grandmother would have liked that very much."

"MY grandmother?" She said,

"Did you know MY grandmother?"

"Of course, I knew her very well! In fact, I helped her run the factory. For three generations we mice were in charge here. We made lots of good things to eat—peach orange clove jam, pepper jelly, cakes and sweets. The jam and jelly factory was such a happy place to be. We loved working here."

He shut his eyes as a tear escaped and said, "But alas, that was many years ago. Now look at us. Everything is overgrown and inside the factory it feels so gloomy!"

Then his face brightened as he explained, "We do the very best we can—and I keep hoping . . ."

Mr. Jam put his pipe to his mouth and hung his head.

Rowena felt very sorry for the old mouse, but she was still excited about going inside. She remembered how wonderful it had been many years ago, when she had spent a summer visiting her grandmother. She could not wait to see it again.

She pushed the door open and followed Mr. Jam inside. They had entered the front room which was also a store.

Mr. Jam showed Rowena the fireplace against the far wall. He also pointed to his own small home nearby as he hung his hat on the hook. In the dim light she could see the sofa where she knew her grandmother had spent many hours sitting with her friends having Sunshine Fruit Tea and Pinwheel Sandwiches. Grandmother Rowena always visited with them when they came to buy good things to eat.

What a special place this had been!

But now there were cobwebs everywhere and it was so dusty and dark. Just one little ray of sunlight shown through the overgrown window. How sad, how sad!

"What about the kitchen?" asked Rowena. "Is it all right?"

Poking her head through the door, Rowena gazed about the kitchen. What she saw made her feel even worse. All the machinery was dull and dirty and had the most unhappy look.

"Oh," she said, "This is terrible. I can't let this
be. I must do something. But what...???!!!
    She glanced at Mr. Jam for help, but he looked as
unhappy as the machines.

Suddenly he said, "Wait a minute. I know! Your grandmother's chef's hat! It had something magical about it. When she put it on the most wonderful tastes came out of the machines. It must be here somewhere. Help me look."

Rowena and Mr. Jam looked everywhere—in the cupboards, under the machines, behind the stoves and even in the refrigerator.

While searching near the shelves, Rowena came to a halt. On the wall was a big red button with a sign over it.

Standing on tippy toe Rowena brushed off part of the sign and saw the word "TOUCH." She reached up to press the button.

Mr. Jam yelled, "Don't, Rowena!"

But it was too late! The hidden trap door on which she stood opened and Rowena disappeared.

"Ohhh my," said Mr. Jam, "Rowena, Rowena, are you all right?"

"Yes, I think so," a weak voice answered.

Mr. Jam, ran to the edge of the hole and peered over. There was Rowena on the floor below, covered with cobwebs and coal dust.

Mr. Jam said, "Rowena, you won't find your grandmother's hat there—that's the coal bin! This is where we stored the coal for heating the factory."

The old mouse reached down to help her. Shaking his head he said, "Rowena, you must be more careful. You could get hurt pushing buttons that say "DO NOT TOUCH.""

"DO NOT TOUCH! I thought it said 'TOUCH.' You are right, Mr. Jam. I'll be more careful next time. Don't worry about me. Let's find the hat."

Rowena bent over to brush herself off. Suddenly she let out a whoop of joy!

"I think I see the hat! There it is. It's way back there in the corner behind the sink. It must have fallen there a long time ago."

Running over to the sink, she picked the chef's hat up and dusted it off.

"It looks all right, just a little dirty. Do you really think it might work for me, too? I'm going to try it on right now."

Rowena raised it above her head, shut her eyes tightly and put the hat on. She crossed her fingers for extra luck.

"Will it work? Will the factory come to life again?"

Opening her eyes, Rowena looked all around. EVERYTHING was the same! NOTHING had changed!

The tears started welling up in Rowena's eyes.

"I knew it. There's nothing we can do. The Wonderful Jam and Jelly Factory will never be wonderful again." She felt very alone.

Then Rowena felt something brush her hand. It was Mr. Jam's tiny paw, reaching up to her.

"You mustn't give up," he said. "I have one more idea—your grandmother's cookbook. She carried it with her everywhere. Maybe it's the answer. We must look for it."

Mr. Jam dashed out of the kitchen into the next room. This had been her grandmother's office. There were papers everywhere—boxes full of papers—scraps of fabric, labels, catalogs and old mail piled high. Surely the cookbook must be here somewhere. If only they could find it.

Rowena and Mr. Jam searched through the boxes, inside the bookshelves, under the table and then headed for her grandmother's desk.

They looked on top of the desk, behind it and under it.

Then the two detectives started opening all the drawers. They checked each one carefully and finally reached the very last drawer. It was LOCKED!

"That must mean that there is something important inside," exclaimed Rowena. "How can we get in? We haven't seen a key anywhere!"

Mr. Jellyfords Jam III
jumped up and began to
dance a little jig.

"Wait! Wait! I remember now!" he
said. I found a key years ago and was
afraid to throw it away. Maybe it will fit this drawer."

Mr. Jam disappeared around a corner and came back
dragging a large key. Rowena reached down and took
the key. Gently she tried it in the drawer. IT
WORKED!

Holding her breath, she opened the drawer slowly
and reached in. At first she thought it was empty. But
toward the back of the drawer she touched something
very large. This had to be her grandmother's cookbook.

Carefully Rowena took it out of the place where it
had been safe all these years.

She hugged this treasure to her chest. Was
this the answer? Could she make the factory
come alive again now?

She was certainly going to try. After all, she had Mr. Jellyfords Jam III as her friend. Together they had found her grandmother's hat and cookbook.

Clutching the book tightly, Rowena walked back into the kitchen with Mr. Jam close at her heels.

She reached up and adjusted the chef's hat squarely on her head. Rowena opened the cookbook and started reading out loud. She read the recipe for Fruit Jellies... then the recipe for Thick and Quick Jam... then Peach Orange Crisp... She was really afraid to stop reading. She was even more afraid to look up at everything in the kitchen.

Suddenly she heard Mr. Jam shout. "Rowena! Rowena! LOOK! LOOK! You must look!"

She stopped reading and looked down at Mr. Jam. Rowena knew something wonderful had happened.

There, right in front of her eyes, every machine was shining with happiness. She couldn't believe it. They had done it. The factory was coming to life again.

Rowena grabbed Mr. Jam's paw and they raced to watch the machines work. The dishwasher was merrily swooshing water around in circles, cleaning the jars. The steam kettles were whistling and flapping their tops.

All of a sudden there were worker mice everywhere, putting berries and sugar into the kettles.

They were busy measuring, pouring and stirring all the ingredients that would make those delicious jams and jellies. A little of this! . . . A little of that! That's the fun and the magic of cooking.

Rowena turned around to look for Mr. Jam. He was by the stoves, sampling some of the first batches of jam that the busy mice and machines were producing.

"Hurry, Rowena," called Mr. Jam. "We must put the hopper on the filling machine. The jam is ready to be poured into the jars."

He scooted across the table and helped her place the hopper above the filler. Then all the factory mice began carrying the buckets of jam up the ladder to the top of the hopper.

Mr. Jam was at the top of the ladder. He grabbed the first bucket to empty it into the hopper when suddenly he slipped!

"Oh! Oh! Help! Help! I'm falling!"

KERPLUNK —right into the hopper!
"Save me, Rowena!" All the factory mice were so upset. Only Rowena could help him.

Rowena dashed up to the hopper and peeked over it. There was Mr. Jellyfords Jam III lying at the bottom of the hopper. He had landed in the middle of all that sticky jam. There he sat with a bucket on his head. He looked so undignified and discombobulated that Rowena wanted to laugh out loud.

Trying not to laugh, Rowena reached down and scooped him out. She helped him to the sink to rinse off.

Sputtering a little, a very wet Mr. Jam adjusted his spectacles. He knocked some jam out of his pipe and sat down on the floor for a minute to rest.

Rowena sank down beside Mr. Jam and hugged him with all of her might.

"It's all right. We have done it! The good smells are back and the machines are busy making lots of delicious things to eat."

Rowena was so HAPPY!

She had made the Wonderful Jam and Jelly Factory come alive again.

THE END

ROWENA'S

ADVENTURES IN COOKING

Rowena has chosen some of her very favorite recipes to share with you. In the Jam and Jelly Factory, they make lots of jams and jellies. Rowena has recipes for a jam and a jelly that you can make for yourself. She has included the recipes for her favorite luncheon menu and her grandmother's very favorite menu, too.

Rowena hopes everyone will enjoy the treats you fix, but most of all she hopes you have as much fun cooking as she does. Learning to cook should be fun and always an adventure!

HERE ARE A FEW IMPORTANT RULES TO REMEMBER:

1. Cook only with permission from an adult.
2. Read your recipe carefully before beginning to cook.
3. Get adult help with hot pans.
4. Be sure to use oven mitts when handling hot pans and jars.
5. Be careful around hot burners and ovens.
6. Be careful when using sharp knives.
7. Be sure to clean up the kitchen as you finish each recipe.
8. HAVE FUN!!!

FOR ADULTS TO READ !!

ROWENA'S FAVORITE LUNCH	GRANDMOTHER'S SPECIAL LUNCH
EASY CHILI WITH BOWLS	PINWHEEL SANDWICHES
COLORFUL STRIPS & DIP	SWEETNESS SALAD
FABULOUS FUN –	SUNSHINE FRUIT TEA
FRUIT DRINKS	PEACH-ORANGE CRISP
SHORTBREAD PIZZA	

FRUIT JELLIES

- *MAKES 4 EIGHT OUNCE JARS*
- YOU WILL NEED:

  a large saucepan
  a wooden spoon
  a measuring cup
  a slotted spoon (a spoon with holes in it)
  4 eight ounce jelly jars with lids

  1 can (6 ounce) frozen fruit juice (grape,
     cranberry, or tropical fruit mix)
  1 package (1¾ ounce) powdered
     fruit pectin
  2 cups water
  3¾ cups sugar

1. Thaw the fruit juice. In a saucepan mix juice, fruit pectin and water until dissolved. Heat mixture in saucepan over high heat on burner. Stir constantly for about 2 minutes.
2. When the mixture comes to a rolling boil, slowly add the sugar and heat again until a rolling boil. Boil 1 minute then remove saucepan from the heat. There should be a foam covering the top of saucepan. Skim this foam off with a slotted spoon.
3. To prepare the jars for the jelly, with ADULT HELP, pour very hot water into the jars you plan to use. Make sure that the lids are clean.
4. With ADULT HELP, empty the water from the jars and fill with the jelly. Cover each jar with a tight fitting lid. Cool jelly jars completely and store in refrigerator.

Please be very careful. This mixture is very hot and could burn you. Remember, the jars will be hot too!

THICK AND QUICK JAM

- *MAKES 3 EIGHT OUNCE JARS*
- YOU WILL NEED:

  a large saucepan
  a measuring cup
  a measuring spoon
  a wooden spoon
  3 eight ounce jars with lids

  1 20 ounce package of frozen fruit
     (blueberries, raspberries or
     strawberries)
  2 tablespoons lemon juice
  1 package (1¾ ounce) fruit pectin
  2½ cups sugar

1. In a saucepan, mix fruit and lemon juice over high heat. Cook 2 minutes.
2. Add pectin and heat to a rolling boil, stirring often. Boil 1 minute.
3. Add the sugar and heat again to a rolling boil. Stir often. Boil 1 minute. Remove from heat.
4. To prepare the jars for the jam, with ADULT HELP, pour very hot water into the jars you plan to use. Make sure that the lids are clean.
5. With ADULT HELP, empty the water from the jars and fill them with the jam. Cover completely and store in the refrigerator.

Please be very careful. This mixture is very hot and could burn you. Remember, the jars will be hot too!

EASY CHILI WITH BOWLS

- *MAKES 8 BIG BOWLS*
- YOU WILL NEED:

  a medium saucepan with top
  a wooden spoon
  a can opener
  measuring spoons
  a sharp knife

  1½ pounds ground beef
  1 large onion, chopped
  ¼ teaspoon minced garlic
  1 pound can whole tomatoes
  1 pound can kidney beans
  1 8 ounce can tomato sauce
  1 or 2 tablespoons chili powder
  ½ teaspoon oregano
  grated cheese

1. Cook the ground beef, onions and garlic together over medium heat in a medium size saucepan, until all the red is gone from the meat. Stir carefully! When meat is done, have an ADULT HELP drain the fat.
2. Now add the tomatoes, kidney beans, tomato sauce, chili powder and oregano. Stir well. Cover the saucepan and turn the heat to low. Stir often and cook about 1 hour.
3. Serve in tortilla bowls and top with grated cheese.
4. EAT YOUR BOWL WITH YOUR CHILI!

BOWLS FOR CHILI

- YOU WILL NEED:

  oven proof bowls
  aluminum foil
  pot holders

  1 package 10″ flour tortillas
  butter

1. Preheat oven to 325 degrees.
2. Lightly butter as many tortillas as needed. Stack the tortillas and wrap them in aluminum foil. Heat for 10 minutes in oven. Remove from the oven and they will be soft. Using oven proof bowls, place the soft tortilla inside the bowl, shaping to fit the bowl. Put them back in the oven for 15 minutes or until the tortillas begin to get crisp.
3. Keep the tortillas in the bowl and fill with chili.
4. EAT YOUR CHILI WITH YOUR BOWL!!

COLORFUL STRIPS & DIP

- *MAKES 6 SERVINGS*
- YOU WILL NEED:

  a sharp knife
  cutting board
  one medium size bowl
  stirring spoon
  measuring spoon
  measuring cup

  2 large carrots
  2 stalks celery
  1 small head broccoli
  1 red pepper
  1 green pepper

1. Wash all the vegetables very carefully and pat dry.
2. With the help of an ADULT cut each vegetable into strips on the cutting board. Thin 4″ strips will be best for dipping.
3. Put all the vegetables into a bowl of icy water to keep crisp.

DIP

- YOU WILL NEED:

  ½ cup mayonnaise
  1 tablespoon worcestershire sauce
  ½ cup ketsup
  2-3 drops hot sauce
  ¼ teaspoon onion salt
  ½ teaspoon minced garlic

1. Mix all the ingredients together in a bowl. Chill until ready to serve.
2. Drain your vegetables from the icy water. Arrange the vegetables in a circle on the plate. Place dip in a small bowl in the center of the vegetables. You are ready for a good snack!

This dip is also good with chips or small sausages!

FABULOUS FUN FRUIT DRINKS

- *MAKES ONE DRINK OR MORE*
- YOU WILL NEED:

  tall glasses
  a knife
  a cutting board

  Try—
  Pineapple chunks in cranberry juice
  Banana slices in orange juice
  Seedless white grapes in grape juice
  Melon balls in lemonade
  Blueberries in limeade

This recipe lets you use your imagination! See how many fun combinations you can make with fruit juice and real fruit.
1. Wash fresh fruit carefully and pat dry.
2. Place fruit on a cutting board and VERY CAREFULLY cut into small, bite size pieces.
3. Drop small pieces of fruit into a tall glass and pour in your favorite fruit juice.
4. Add some ice and a drinking straw and ENJOY!

Got the idea? Now mix and match up your own combinations. Cooking should be creative!

SHORTBREAD PIZZA

- *MAKES ONE 9″ PIZZA*
- YOU WILL NEED:

  a large bowl
  a large cookie sheet or
  a pizza pan
  a measuring cup
  clean hands
  spreading knife
  pot holders

  1 cup softened butter
  2 cups flour
  ½ cup confectioner's sugar
  8 tablespoons Lemon Curd or any
      flavored jam
  optional sliced fruit—strawberries, grapes,
      blueberries, any kind of fruit you like

1. Preheat oven to 350 degrees.
2. Combine the butter, flour and sugar and shape into a 9 inch flat circle on a large cookie sheet or pizza pan.
3. Bake 25-30 minutes until lightly browned.
4. While still warm, slide the crust onto a serving platter. Spread with 8 tablespoons of Lemon Curd or jam.
5. It's great now but it's even better if you decorate it with sliced fruit. So pretty! Cut it into wedges to serve. So good!!

PINWHEEL SANDWICHES

- *MAKES 8-12 SANDWICHES*
- YOU WILL NEED:

  a sharp knife
  a rolling pin
  a spreading knife

  1 loaf of unsliced bread
  peanut butter or cream cheese
  raisins
  fruit jelly or Thick & Quick Jam

1. With an ADULT'S HELP cut the crust off the bread. Now slice the bread horizontally into ¼ inch slices.
2. With a rolling pin, flatten each slice. Spread with peanut butter, jam and sprinkle with raisins. Start at one short end and roll up.
3. Wrap each roll in plastic wrap and refrigerate 1 hour. Slice each roll into the number of sandwiches you will need.

SWEETNESS SALAD

- *MAKES 4-6 SERVINGS*
- YOU WILL NEED:

  a medium size bowl
  a measuring cup
  measuring spoons
  a sharp knife

  1 apple
  1 bunch of seedless grapes
  ½ cup berries (strawberries,
    blueberries, or raspberries)
  1 banana
  2 tablespoons orange juice
  1 tablespoon Thick & Quick Jam
    or honey

1. Rinse all the fruit very well.
2. Cut the apple in half and put the cut side down on a cutting board. Make 4 wedges with each half. Cut each wedge into 4 bite size pieces. Put the apple pieces, grapes and berries in a bowl.
3. Peel the banana and slice into bite size pieces. Add pieces to rest of the fruit in the bowl.
4. Mix the orange juice with the jam or honey in a small bowl.
5. Pour mixture over the fruit.
6. Chill in the refrigerator until ready to eat.

SUNSHINE FRUIT TEA

- *MAKES 4-5 CUPS*
- YOU WILL NEED:

  a measuring cup
  a sharp knife
  a teapot or covered pitcher
  tea cups or glasses

  5 cups of water
  1 lemon or lime
  1 tangerine or orange
  1 family size tea bag or
  4 small tea bags
  dash of cinnamon, allspice and cloves

1. Heat 5 cups of water to boiling.
2. While water is getting hot, cut lemon or lime and the tangerine or orange into 4 slices. Put ½ of each kind of fruit in the teapot. Add the teabag and spices to the pot.
3. When the water comes to a boil carefully pour it over the fruit and spices in the teapot. Cover the pot and let it stand for 5 minutes. Take out the tea bags and fruit.
4. Cut the rest of the fruit in half and place in the tea cups. Pour the tea into the cups. Add honey or sugar to sweeten the tea.
5. This tea can also be served in a glass with ice.

PEACH-ORANGE CRISP

- *MAKES 6-8 SERVINGS*
- YOU WILL NEED:

  a 1 quart baking dish
  a measuring cup
  measuring spoons
  a mixing bowl
  a fork
  pot holders

  1 jar (8 ounce) Rowena's Peach-Orange
      Clove Jam or any peach flavored jam
  1 tablespoon lemon juice
  3 tablespoons water
  1 egg
  1 cup all-purpose flour
  1 cup sugar
  4 tablespoons melted butter

1. Preheat oven to 350 degrees.
2. Grease a 1 quart baking dish.
3. Spread the jar of jam all over the bottom
   of the baking dish.
4. Sprinkle the jam with lemon juice and
   water.
5. In a separate bowl, beat the egg and add
   the flour and sugar. Mix with a fork
   until crumbly.
6. Sprinkle the crumbs over the peach jam.
   Drizzle the melted butter over the
   crumbs.
7. Place dish in the oven and bake 30-35
   minutes.
8. Serve warm and for an extra treat—top
   with your favorite ice cream!